THE SILVER PENDAxNT

Haeworth Robertson

Venture Books
Washington, DC

To purchase this book online, please refer to
www.silverpendantmystery.com

Printed and bound in Canada by Art Bookbindery

ISBN 978-0-615-34153-8

for
Maria

Bill & Judy
with thanks
for your help.
Haworth
April 8, 2010

Contents

1. The Drowning   9

2. The Rapid Descent   11

3. The Actuary   17

4. The Employer   23

5. The Investment Company   27

6. The Financier   33

7. The Dancer   39

8. The Shopping List   45

9. The Missing Link   53

10. The Retribution   57

11. The Analysis   61

12. The Response   65

13. The Official Story   71

14. Epilogue   75

THE SILVER PENDAxNT

Adventure is nothing but a romantic name for trouble.
—Louis L'Amour

1.

The Drowning

Scott Martin couldn't hold his breath any longer. Water started filling his nostrils, slowly at first and then in a big rush. He was drowning. He had known he was going to die but not like this.

Two months earlier he had moved into the Potomac Nursing Home, a clinic that specialized in caring for patients with AIDS. His treatments, which had been somewhat unorthodox, were so successful that it appeared he might live much longer than his doctors had originally thought.

Scott had been looking forward to today when his sister was to visit him. It was even possible that she might arrange for him to return home to a fairly normal life. His attendant had rolled him in his wheelchair out on the lawn at the top of a hill overlooking the Potomac River, just twenty yards below. His sister should be there any minute and he was relaxed, enjoying the warm sunshine.

Suddenly, a nearby fellow patient cried out for help and Scott's attendant rushed to his aid. At that moment, Scott's wheelchair started rolling down the hill and before anyone noticed he was sliding into the Potomac—cheated, at age 30, of the rest of his life.

2.

The Rapid Descent

Jimmy Jackson had been planning this vacation for more than a year: A hike down to the floor of the Grand Canyon, one night in a bunkhouse at Phantom Ranch, then a five-day raft trip through the rapids of the Colorado River, sleeping at night in the open air on the riverbank. A challenging and romantic adventure.

National Park authorities limit the number of entrants into the Park each summer, so reservations have to be made months in advance and there is a waiting list of prospective hikers. Jimmy had organized the trip, originally planning to go with three of his bowling buddies. One of them had dropped out, however, and the Park authorities had asked if Jimmy would allow someone on the waiting list to fill the slot. Jimmy had agreed and his group was joined by a stranger. One who looked tough enough to make the trip and gave only a single name—Tony—and kept his conversation to a minimum.

Over dinner at the El Tovar Lodge dining room the night before the hike, the foursome had debated which of the two trails they should take down to Phantom Ranch. Both were tortuous trails descending to a depth of a mile below the canyon rim. The South Kaibab Trail was only 6.5 miles long but was the tougher one—dangerously steep, no water available anywhere along the trail and almost nothing in the way of shade. Jimmy was easily fatigued these days and he persuaded the group to take the easier Bright Angel Trail, although it was almost ten miles long.

At six o'clock the next morning they set out. It was mid-July, on what promised to be a hot, nearly cloudless day—one that would test their stamina. Their intent was to stick together in case of an emergency. However, at Two Mile Corner, Jimmy and Tony lagged behind to inspect some petroglyphs on the walls above the trail. They all met up at Indian Garden, almost midway in their journey. Indian Garden had trees, water, and even picnic tables. It also had park rangers to administer electrolyte drinks and other aid to weary travelers.

After lunch Tony said he wanted to take a side trip down the trail leading to Plateau Point, which he had heard has an awesome view of the Inner Gorge and the Colorado River—and of their ultimate destination, Phantom Ranch. Jimmy agreed to go with him but the other two decided to proceed directly to Phantom Ranch. It was only an extra three miles roundtrip to Plateau Point, but they thought a ten-mile hike was enough for one day.

The Plateau Point Trail is on relatively flat ground but there is no shade, and this was in the middle of the day. Jimmy was tired and thirsty by the time they reached the Point—an overlook almost 800 feet straight down. Tony positioned himself on a boulder at the edge of the cliff and had Jimmy take his photo. He then offered to take Jimmy's photo at the same spot. Jimmy was still a little light-headed from heat exhaustion but, good sport that he was, he climbed up on the boulder and posed for the last photo that would ever be taken of him. Jimmy wasn't sure how it happened but he suddenly found himself alternately falling through space and crashing into the walls of the cliff.

When dinner was served that night at Phantom Ranch, neither Jimmy nor Tony was present. Jimmy's two friends were not too worried but they were concerned enough to report Jimmy and Tony as overdue. It was not until the next day that

Jimmy's body was found halfway down the cliff from Plateau Point.

It would probably have taken weeks to find him except that, in an overabundance of caution, Jimmy had bought a Personal Locator Beacon just for this trip. When activated, these devices continuously broadcast one's latitude and longitude and are increasingly used by hikers and adventurers as a precaution against getting lost. The rescuers had not been able to tell how this "accident" had happened. And Tony was not around to shed any light on it.

3.

The Actuary

Alan Jameson had the full attention of his students as he told the story of how a Greek philosopher and mathematician had calculated the circumference of the earth, just by using his reasoning powers and simple mathematics.

Pacing enthusiastically back and forth, Alan brought to life a vision of Eratosthenes, born in 276 B.C.E. in Cyrene in modern Libya. Educated in Athens and Alexandria, at age 40 he was appointed head of the Great Library at Alexandria, the center of science and learning in the ancient world. At age 36 he had observed that at noontime of the summer solstice, the sun shone directly overhead in Syene (now Aswan in southern Egypt) yet cast a shadow of the Alexandria Spire in his hometown of Alexandria. Based on the length of the shadow, the height of the Spire, and the distance from Syene to Alexandria, Eratosthenes used simple ratios to estimate the circumference of the Earth—and he was off by less than one percent.

Alan Jameson was not an historian; he was a mathematics teacher. But he always tried to demonstrate how the mathematical principles being studied could be used to solve some real life problem—instead of being just an abstract exercise. He had heard that several of his students were considering becoming teachers as a result of his enthusiasm and easy manner in presenting his lessons.

At Virginia State University he had majored in mathematics and taken a few education courses. Math, in particular, had seemed easy. Most of the time it seemed logical, rational. Not something you could say about some of the social sciences. Besides, not many people liked math so his attraction to it set him apart. Upon graduation, he had taken a job as a mathematics teacher in a private high school in the Virginia suburbs of Washington, DC.

Alan was a good teacher. He prepared his lessons thoroughly. He graded each student's homework and examinations carefully, annotating them to explain where the student could have improved. But it was his physical presence that gave him a big advantage over most of the other teachers. At six feet tall, with blond wavy hair and an athletic build, he was truly handsome. Still, that wasn't his main advantage. He had taken only one college class in public speaking but his professor had noted that for some reason he couldn't explain, when Alan walked to the front of the classroom and began to speak, his classmates became very quiet and listened—not something they did for everyone.

When Alan was growing up his father had always expected him to do his best, and that's the way he treated his students. His conscientious efforts paid off: Most of his students showed a real interest in mathematics—not usually a student's favorite subject—and in his second year of teaching he was voted his school's "teacher of the year."

For a while, then, everything seemed good. The pay was a little low but he wasn't married and didn't need much. Repaying his student loans was beginning to be a burden, however. Also, it was beginning to bother him that he was paid so little to teach his already privileged students how to go into the business world and earn what seemed like obscene salaries. He remembered once reading that the top ten earners of an investment firm had averaged $40 million each in the year before their firm had failed. Was their work really worth a thousand times the value of his work?

Alan Jameson had decided to make a career move that he hoped would change his life.

In searching for another way to use his analytic talents, Alan had learned about actuaries. The actuarial profession had its beginnings in the late 18th century in Great Britain when newly formed life insurance companies sought a scientific basis on which to provide life insurance. The first actuaries used mathematical probabilities and statistics to determine proper life insurance premiums and reserves. As time went by, the actuarial profession expanded to deal with government insurance programs and pension plans, as well as other forms of insurance.

A recent edition of *The Jobs Rated Almanac* had rated the profession of actuary as number one in the country based on six primary components of job quality: income, physical demands, environment, outlook, security, and stress. The major disadvantage seemed to be that it would require several years and thousands of hours of self-study to become a fully qualified actuary. But he didn't mind that; Alan liked to study and learn. Besides, this would be another way to set himself apart from the rest of the crowd.

So, in his spare time Alan began studying and taking the examinations required to become an accredited actuary. He progressed rapidly because of his mathematical background, and after three years had qualified as an Associate of the Society of Actuaries. He still had a few years to go before attaining full qualification as a Fellow of the Society of Actuaries; however, his training was sufficient to make a career change and join the actuarial staff of a life insurance company.

4.

The Employer

Alan Jameson, Assistant Actuary of DC Capital Life Insurance Company in Washington, DC. It sounded pretty good. He had selected this company partly because he already lived in the area and partly because of its training program. For the first two years he would work six months at a time in each of four departments.

His first assignment was in the underwriting department. Here, the applications for insurance were reviewed and premium rates were assigned according to the risk category of each individual. The risk categories were based on the applicant's age, sex, medical history, occupation, lifestyle (skydiving was not good, for example), and a few other factors.

After six months Alan was transferred to the actuarial department and assigned to a small team studying the company's mortality experience.

The company's mortality experience had been deteriorating recently. For the past five years, almost twice as many deaths had occurred as had been expected based on the various factors used to determine premium rates—even after adjusting for the increase because of AIDS-related deaths. This was a much greater variation from the norm than was reasonable, and it was the job of the team Alan was on to find out why.

Actually, Alan thought of it as his personal responsibility—not the team's—to resolve this problem. The team had no formal leader, but Alan had a presence that usually resulted in his being the *de facto* leader of any team he was a part of. In fact, he found it hard to get really involved in a project unless he assumed that role.

5.

The Investment Company

Frederick F. Fox, or Freddy as he was called before he started his investment company, had worked 15 years for DC Capital Life Insurance Company. He had been an underwriter, so he knew almost everything about people who bought insurance from DC Capital when he worked there.

When he was growing up, his classmates had called him "foxy" and had taunted him with the phrase "sly as a fox." Yet he had never really lived up to that descriptor and seemed to be stuck in a routine job at DC Capital with little prospect for advancement. It was beginning to bother

Freddy that most of the applicants for insurance that he reviewed were leading a richer lifestyle than he was.

Then one day Freddy had an epiphany: an idea for a business venture that would enable him to be his own boss and that could make him rich. It came to him as a result of consolidating three pieces of information.

First, DC Capital was licensed to sell insurance only in Washington, DC. And since DC had a large gay community and several of DC Capital's insurance agents were gay, a significant portion of DC Capital's policyholders was gay.

Second, in June 1981 the first AIDS cases were reported in America. By 1987, more than 50,000 people—predominantly gay males between ages 20 and 50—had been diagnosed as HIV-positive. And since Washington, DC had America's highest HIV/AIDS infection rate, an increasing number of DC Capital's policyholders had

AIDS and were given only a short time to live—and they badly needed money for living expenses and medical treatment.

Third, when reading about the early history of the life insurance business, Freddy learned that Elizur Wright—often called the father of American life insurance—went to England in 1844 on a business trip doing research for Massachusetts Hospital Life Insurance Company. And while visiting the Royal Exchange in London, Wright had witnessed the auctioning of life insurance policies of impoverished men who were unable to continue paying premiums on them.

Thus, Freddy Fox conceived the idea of an investment company that would buy insurance policies from persons who were terminally or chronically ill and who needed money for living and medical expenses now, not after they died. The investment company would pay the insured an immediate lump sum and would then pay future premiums on the policy and collect the future death benefits. Frederick F. Fox would soon organize and become the president of Fox Investments, whose investments would be known as "viatical settlements."

One of Fox Investment's first viatical settlements would involve Scott Martin, the drowning victim. When Scott was aged 22, he had bought a $200,000 whole life insurance policy and designated his younger sister as beneficiary. The premiums for this insurance policy were $155 per month, payable until his death, at which time $200,000 would be paid to his beneficiary. The insurance policy had a "double indemnity" provision, so that $400,000 would be paid if his death were accidental.

At age 27, Scott was diagnosed with AIDS and given two years to live. For medical bills and living expenses, he needed money now and his main asset was his life insurance policy.

Since he couldn't work any longer, he couldn't afford to keep paying premiums; therefore, he could either cancel the policy and get a cash surrender value of $4,017 from the insurance company, or sell his policy to a company like Fox Investments for $130,000. Fox Investments would pay the future premiums and receive the $200,000 (or $400,000) death benefit when it was paid. Since Fox Investments expected the policyholder to die within about two years, it anticipated a handsome return on its investment. Scott received, in effect, an advance on his death benefit.

Before he sold his insurance policy, however, Scott Martin asked why Fox Investments would pay him $130,000, while DC Capital would pay him only $4,017 as a cash surrender value. The Fox Investment agent explained that the cash surrender value offered by a life insurance company depended on factors determined at the time a policy was issued and did not take into account any subsequent changes in the insured's health. In contrast, Fox Investment's offer depended on a current evaluation of the insured's health and the resulting life expectancy estimate.

While Scott didn't completely understand all this, he was able to put his doubts aside since he was going to receive $130,000 instead of $4,017.

In fact, Freddy Fox had designed a completely legitimate business plan, fair to all parties, provided only that all the calculations were made appropriately and in good faith.

6.

The Financier

Anthony "Tony" Roselle owned one of the most profitable gentlemen's clubs in Washington, DC—*Tony's Club*, a nude dancing bar. Different parts of the country have different dress codes, but in DC the only requirement is that the dancers wear shoes. Of course they all wear garters so the wide-eyed customers will have some place to put their dollars as they analyze each dancer's anatomy. It's sort of an ultimate peep show. Instead of inserting a coin in a machine and ogling a photo, you insert a dollar bill in a garter and see the real thing—up close.

When Freddy Fox was still an underwriter for DC Capital, he considered his job to be pretty boring. And his sex life wasn't much better. He was married to a good, steady woman who was attractive in her own way but there was not much excitement there. He had stopped by *Tony's Club* after work one night and had found the change of pace surprisingly relaxing. The music was too loud and the lyrics pretty gross at times, but he really enjoyed seeing the wide variety of female figures—every size, shape and hue. He had his favorites, of course, but he tipped them all just as a matter of courtesy.

He had been going to *Tony's* for several years now and occasionally talked with Tony and some of the girls, many of whom he knew by name—stage name, at least. The bartender knew him and had his favorite drink on the bar before he even sat down. Some nights he barely looked at the dancers. They and the music just formed the background for his musings. It was on one of those nights that his thoughts about forming Fox Investments coalesced. He had it all planned out, except for how to get the financial backing such a venture would need.

Tony's Club was largely a cash business and provided ample opportunities to hide money from the Internal Revenue Service. Surprisingly, however, *Tony's* always reported an abnormally large profit. Some said he was laundering money for the mob. With all this money floating around, Tony was always on the lookout for a profitable investment. So when Freddy told him about his dreams for Fox Investments, Tony was uncommonly interested. He immediately saw opportunities to increase Fox Investment's profits that Freddy Fox had never thought of.

Although Freddy didn't have much business experience, he sensed that Tony was not the most desirable person to be in business with. However, Freddy didn't have many contacts with access to money, particularly for such a new and speculative venture. So, Tony became a major investor in Fox Investments, as a silent partner.

Freddy rounded up several other investors so that undue control of the company would not rest with any one investor, particularly Tony. When word of Freddy's plans got out, a surprising party expressed interest in making a small investment in Fox Investments: Tucker Carlton III, president and founder of DC Capital Life Insurance Company.

Mr. Carlton was a pillar of the community, active in civic affairs and a local philanthropist. As an astute—if somewhat unethical—businessman, he had secretly sold most of his stock in DC Capital after reading a confidential internal memo stating that an anticipated increase in AIDS-related death claims would cost DC Capital dearly. Now he saw that Fox Investments offered a way to make DC Capital's loss his gain. From Freddy's viewpoint, having Mr. Carlton as an investor would lend much-needed credibility to his venture.

7.

The Dancer

Maria Olsen was true to her Scandinavian heritage. Tall, long blond hair, green eyes, slim yet well-rounded, and when she gave you that "come-hither" look you thought you were the only man in the room. If she wanted to, she could have easily been a *Playboy* Playmate of the Year.

She had danced at *Tony's Club* for five years—part time for four years while working her way through college, and then full time. Maria was a good student and could easily make good in the business world using only her brains, but using her beauty was more financially rewarding and she had been reluctant to give up dancing.

When Maria moved from Ely, Minnesota to Washington, DC to attend college, nude dancing was the farthest thing from her mind. It was her college roommate who persuaded her that it was okay—that and her need for spending money. Washington had proved to be more expensive than she had planned for. Her roommate also convinced her that nude dancers were not the ones being taken advantage of; it was the men who were being exploited. Still, from Maria's standpoint there was a stigma attached to exhibiting oneself to a stranger. It was certainly not something to write home about.

Then one night Tony had approached her with a proposition almost too good to be true. Would she like to cut her dancing schedule back to two days a week and work full-time as special assistant to Freddy Fox at Fox Investments? In addition to her regular salary at Fox Investments, she would receive a substantial bonus—under the table—from Tony, as well as her earnings as a dancer. Tony explained that he had made a large investment in Fox Investments several years earlier and wanted someone to keep an eye on what was happening there. Nothing illegal or dangerous, just keep an eye on things. Because of his investment in Fox, it was easy for Tony to place Maria in this job with Freddy.

Maria was thrilled at the opportunity to start moving away from the sometimes sleazy world of nude dancing and into the business world. There was only one thing she didn't like about all this: Tony had asked that she get her body pierced as part of the deal. Maria took pride in her beautiful body, unmarred by tattoos or piercings, and couldn't understand why Tony would request this. Maybe, she reasoned, it was just because most of the other dancers had piercings. In any event, it wasn't a big deal and she couldn't pass up this opportunity so she agreed. Besides, Tony wasn't the kind of man you questioned or talked back to.

Tony wanted the piercing anywhere that wouldn't show when she was dressed normally; otherwise, the location was up to Maria. This ruled out eyebrow, nose, tongue, and labret rings, but Maria thought these were hideous anyway. Nipple rings wouldn't work either since Maria had full, firm breasts with turgid nipples that would make a nipple ring or barbell obvious, especially when she was bra-less, as she often was.

This left belly button or genital piercing. One of the dancers was all in favor of clit hood piercing because it was very stimulating, giving lots of sensation with relatively little pain. She recommended vertical hood piercing since it gave more thrill than horizontal piercing. But Maria decided on belly button piercing since it was a favorite among models and celebrities and thus more socially acceptable. Also because her recessed navel would accommodate it well. Then she chose an assortment of attractive titanium navel rings in an attempt to make the best of the situation.

8.

The Shopping List

Alan Jameson wasn't quite sure where to start on his study of the excessive mortality that DC Capital was experiencing. He began by sorting the death claims into various categories, and found that most of the now-deceased insured persons had several things in common.

- They had been diagnosed with a terminal illness but had outlived their life expectancy.
- They had sold their insurance in a viatical settlement to Fox Investments.
- They had died in an accident.

Alan had never met Freddy Fox, but he knew that Freddy used to work as an underwriter for DC Capital. He had also heard that Freddy maintained contact with several of his old friends at DC Capital. Perhaps it was natural that so many DC Capital policyholders would arrange viatical settlements with Fox Investments, yet there was something disturbing about all these coincidences.

By inquiring around, Alan learned that Freddy had an administrative assistant, Maria Olsen, who danced twice a week at *Tony's Club*. In the old days this would have certainly been frowned upon, but today a little moonlighting seemed acceptable, even as a club dancer. On his first visit to *Tony's Club*, Alan talked casually with some of the girls but was careful to avoid showing any particular interest in Maria.

Tony was not completely surprised to see Alan in his Club. He had heard that Alan had been asking questions about the operations of Fox Investments and Freddy's continuing contacts with DC Capital. Alan had also been asking questions about Maria. Accordingly, Tony instructed Maria to make casual contact with Alan on his next visit to the Club to learn what his interest was in Fox Investments.

So, on Alan's next visit to *Tony's* he was pleasantly surprised to find himself "accidentally" sitting at the bar next to Maria. Maria didn't normally make herself so readily available to the patrons. Her usual routine was to dance on stage for fifteen minutes, collect as many dollar bills as she could entice the oglers to put in her garter and then—only slightly more clothed— make the rounds of the room, greeting everyone with a smile and a handshake, hoping to collect a few more dollars.

House rules didn't permit her to ask a customer directly for a tip or to buy her a drink, but she could extract both of these from anyone she wanted to—she knew how and when to flirt. Occasionally Maria would sit with a customer and try to carry on a conversation—if the customer seemed interesting or was willing to spend freely on drinks and tips. Most nights she would retire to the dressing room to change costumes and read a book while waiting for her next set.

But tonight was different. Maria had a mission and she had managed casually to sit next to Alan at the bar. At first, both of them were guarded in their conversation but before the evening was over they seemed like old friends. Alan suggested that they see each other for dinner the next night, away from *Tony's*, and was surprised that she accepted so readily.

These dinners became more frequent, and before long Alan found himself in Maria's apartment—and in her bed. They had become so intimate that there were moments when both of them forgot they were supposed to be spying on each other. One night Maria let it slip that Tony was not only a large investor in Fox Investments but that he had asked her to assemble what he called a "shopping list" from the confidential files of Fox Investments: a list of DC Capital's policyholders who had sold their insurance policies to Fox Investments, people with large amounts of insurance that included accidental death, or double indemnity, coverage. The list was also to include certain personal information that could only have been obtained from the original insurance files at DC Capital.

Alan expressed mild interest in this shopping list, saying it might be interesting to study the mortality experience of persons who had arranged viatical settlements— the kind of thing that would interest only an actuary. Maria had no idea what the list was for but Tony had emphasized that she should not tell anyone about it, not even Freddy. So, she didn't volunteer to show a copy to Alan, at least for now.

Of course Tony had been keeping tabs on the developing relationship between Maria and Alan, and he was getting a little impatient that Maria had not found out what Alan's motives were in his continuing inquiries about the operations of Fox Investments.

About this time Tony gave Maria a specially designed belly button ring that he said Alan might enjoy. It was a pendant consisting of a silver A_x, the actuarial symbol for the value of a life insurance policy. At a distance only the A was visible so it might be thought to stand for Actuary or even Alan. Tony suggested she wear this pendant when she was with Alan, saying Alan might get a little thrill out of this *double entendre* symbolism.

Maria continually updated Tony's shopping list, and she had decided there would be no harm in showing Alan one of the old lists. Her spying relationship had developed into a genuine caring relationship and she wanted to please Alan. So the next time they met in her apartment, she had two surprises for Alan: an outdated shopping list and a new, shiny pendant in her navel.

First, the pendant. Maria was proud of her body and liked to parade around her apartment, uninhibited and completely naked—except for her belly button ring. Especially when Alan was there to admire her. This usually resulted in a speedy trip to the bedroom and tonight was no exception. After they had settled down and their hearts stopped racing, Maria had presented Alan with the *pièce de résistance* : the shopping list. This evening was almost too much for Alan to bear, and he had gone home in a state of near ecstasy.

9.

The Missing Link

Alan couldn't wait to get to the office the next day to continue his investigation. In fact, he awoke at 3:00 a.m. and showered and shaved and went in early. He needed some extra time alone to try to solve this puzzle, now that he had more of the pieces.

Alan had read widely about all aspects of providing life insurance. One thing that caught his attention was the question of "insurable interest." Today, when an individual buys insurance, the beneficiary who is to receive the death benefit must have an insurable interest in the life of the insured. For example, the beneficiary should be closely related to the insured by blood or by law, or should expect to suffer a financial loss if the insured dies prematurely. In short, the beneficiary should have a substantial interest in the continuing life, health, and bodily safety of the insured.

This principle was established in English common law in the 19th century for an obvious reason: to prevent someone from purchasing insurance on the life of another person and then hastening that person's death.

But even though an insurance company is prohibited from selling insurance to a person where there is no insurable interest, once the insurance policy has been issued it can be resold by the insured to a third party—like Fox Investments—and there is no requirement that an insurable interest exist. There is no requirement that the new owner (who is also the beneficiary) of the insurance policy have a vested interest in the ongoing survival of the insured. In fact, the opposite situation exists: the new owner of the insurance policy would benefit most from the early death of the insured. Could this moral hazard have been a factor in the extraordinary number of deaths—particularly accidental deaths—that DC Capital had been experiencing?

Thus far in his life, Alan Jameson had lived in a kind of ivory tower of academics and professionals so this idea seemed too offensive to entertain. Yet he knew he must give this possibility serious thought.

10.

The Retribution

Alan was energized at the thought of seeing Maria despite an exhausting day at the office. He couldn't wait to tell her what he thought he had discovered—and that she should extricate herself from this whole sordid business as soon as possible, just in case he was correct.

He let himself into her apartment, silently so he could surprise her. He hoped she would be naked and so she was, lying face down on the bed—resting up for their evening's activities, he presumed. He caressed the back of her neck and then gently turned her over so he could kiss her nipples, something she always loved. But this time she didn't respond; Maria wasn't breathing. She looked normal but then he saw the spot of blood on her navel. No belly button ornament. It had been ripped from her navel.

Shocked and alarmed, Alan knew only one thing for sure—he had to hide or get out of town. Remorse over his role in Maria's death would have to wait. Whoever had discovered that Maria had given him the shopping list obviously knew he had it. And if they had silenced Maria, he was next.

He remembered an out-of-the-way place in the Bahamas where he had vacationed when he graduated from college, a place no one knew he had been. He didn't dare return to his apartment so he gathered up a few clothes he kept at Maria's and set out for BWI—Baltimore-Washington International Airport. Better to drive and leave his car at the airport than take a taxi or shuttle—a smaller paper trail. For that same reason he wouldn't be able to use his credit cards and he definitely needed cash. He had accumulated a large amount of cash at his apartment as the threat of terrorism and the need for a fast evacuation from Washington, DC had become more imminent since 9/11, but that wouldn't do him any good now. Then he remembered that Maria had been saving all her tips in a shoe box deep inside her closet. That would be enough.

Alan was able to get on a late-night flight directly from BWI to Nassau. Once in Nassau he took a public bus into town and then walked to the inter-island ferry terminal at Potter's Cay. A short wait and then a three-hour ferry ride to Harbour Island off the east coast of North Eleuthera. From there to the Coral Sands resort with 33 rooms in two buildings located right on the beach. This was not remote enough to hide him permanently, but it should give him a day or so to gather his wits.

11.

The Analysis

After a fitful night's sleep and a hearty island breakfast, Alan went to an isolated stretch of beach, sat in a chair partially shaded by an umbrella, and thought. He always relaxed better when sitting in the sun. Sunshine also increased his libido but that wasn't a factor today. He just wanted to reflect, analyze, and think.

He had three priorities: First, stay alive. Second, find Maria's killer and the killers of the viatical settlement victims—and thus his potential killer. Third, and on a grander scale, figure out how to remove the moral hazard of viatical settlements that could result in future murders.

Alan decided that Tony must be killing off insured persons selected from the shopping list—by accidental means, if possible, to further increase Fox Investment's profits by collecting double indemnity benefits. He assumed that neither Freddy nor Maria was aware of Tony's scheme. They probably should have suspected something, but their financial rewards were too great for them to raise questions.

Tony must have somehow learned that Maria had given Alan the shopping list and concluded that, to forestall further investigation, he must eliminate Maria— and then Alan.

Alan wasn't sure what to do or whom to trust. Then he remembered Tucker Carlton III, who was not only a respected member of the community and president of DC Capital, but also a minor stockholder in

Fox Investments. Surely he could turn to him for help.

So Alan telephoned Mr. Carlton and told him he had some important information about irregularities at Fox Investments that might explain the large number of death claims DC Capital was experiencing. Alan was relieved that instead of dismissing him out of hand, Mr. Carlton had swiftly responded that Alan should stay in place, call no one else, and that he, Carlton, would be there within twelve hours.

12.

The Response

Immediately after Carlton had heard from Alan, he called Tony and told him to bring his passport and gun and meet him as soon as possible at the Leesburg Executive Airport, where DC Capital's corporate jet was based. They met and flew directly to the largest of the three airports on Eleuthera, then chartered a speedboat to take them to Harbour Island.

Nine hours after calling Mr. Carlton, Alan heard a knock on his hotel door. It was Carlton. Right behind him was Tony Roselle.

Alan was totally perplexed. He had called Carlton because he thought Tony had murdered Maria and was going to kill him, and here was Tony—with Carlton. He didn't know what to say and in his bewilderment blurted out that Freddy Fox's assistant, Maria, had been murdered and that he, Alan, was probably a suspect.

Carlton pulled a gun from his pocket and pointed it at Alan's head. With his other hand he produced a navel pendant with a silver A_x, saying that he had silenced Maria himself—smothering her with a pillow. Alan stammered that he thought Tony did it, whereupon Carlton boastfully explained the whole thing. He wouldn't often have the chance to tell anyone how clever he had been; besides, he didn't plan for Alan to be around to repeat the story.

He, Tucker Carlton III, was the brains behind the entire scheme. He was the principal stockholder in Fox Investments and had used Tony as a front, paying him handsomely for his efforts and discretion. He had instructed Tony to place Maria as Freddy's assistant and obtain the shopping list, which Tony then passed on to Carlton. He could have obtained the list directly but he wanted to distance himself from the transaction as much as possible.

When Alan started snooping around, Carlton had instructed Tony to have Maria insinuate herself into Alan's life. He had directed Tony to give Maria a navel pendant with a tiny transmitter to wear when she was with Alan so that, unknown to Maria, Carlton could keep track of their activities. And that, of course, is how Carlton knew Maria had given Alan the shopping list. Finally, Tucker Carlton III said he was not about to have his financial empire destroyed by a go-go dancer and a number-crunching actuary.

Tony had always known he was just a pawn in Carlton's scheme, but it irked him to have it spelled out so clearly—and publicly. And he remembered that pawns were expendable. Nevertheless, when Carlton told Tony they were going to march Alan down to a remote area of the beach, Tony complied. When they reached the beach, Alan tried to stall his execution. He said he still couldn't believe that Carlton was capable of murdering all these people and having it look like an accident.

Carlton proudly recounted the details of a couple of his schemes: The "accidental" drowning of Scott Martin in the Potomac River, and the "accidental" freefall of Jimmy Jackson in the Grand Canyon. In his zeal to sound impressive, Carlton said that to dispose of Jackson he had hired an assassin who called himself Tony and fit the description of Tony Roselle—just in case things didn't go smoothly. Tony, feeling more and more like a helpless pawn, was beginning to seethe inside.

Carlton announced that show-and-tell was over and told Tony to pull out his gun so they could both shoot Alan simultaneously—thus keeping either one from admitting the murder. Without a second thought, Tony whipped a .40-caliber Glock out of his waistband and shouted that he had no knowledge of Carlton's schemes and that he refused to shoot Alan—he then shot Carlton twice in the chest. Carlton's gun reactively fired one shot that sailed out into the ocean. Tony then took Maria's navel pendant from Carlton's pocket and adjusted it some way before putting it in his own pocket.

13.

The Official Story

One more time that night Alan was speechless. Tony said he couldn't control himself. This public humiliation was too much, especially by Carlton—a rich, pompous, hypocritical, immoral, son-of-a-bitch. But now Tony had a serious problem that he related to Alan. As a young man he had served prison time for participating in an armed robbery in which one of his partners had shot and killed a cashier in a convenience store. With that record, if he were tied in any way to Carlton's murder he would surely go back to prison, something he couldn't endure.

He told Alan he could think of only two solutions. He could kill Alan, the only witness, and then try to hide out the rest of his life—something that would be hard to do, not to mention very unpleasant. Or they could say that Alan had discovered Carlton's viatical settlement murder scheme, that Carlton had murdered Maria and had tried to kill Alan to silence him, but that Alan had shot Carlton in self-defense.

Alan doubted this story would hold up, until Tony explained that—unknown to Carlton—Maria's navel pendant not only transmitted but recorded and stored the last hour of every sound it picked up—like a black box recorder on an airplane. Carlton's admissions of guilt and his intention to shoot Alan, as well as Tony's innocence, were recorded on Maria's silver belly button ornament, right up to the point Tony had disabled the recording feature.

So this became the official story. Naturally there were awkward moments, such as explaining why Alan had an unregistered gun in his possession. But all these problems paled in comparison with the terrible crimes that Tucker Carlton III had committed and that were acknowledged on Maria's silver navel pendant. Most everyone who heard the story agreed that justice had been done and that Alan Jameson, actuary, was a hero.

It was time for Alan to take a long vacation on a beach in the sunny Bahamas—but this time on a different island—so he could think, long and hard, about the next chapter in his life.

14.

Epilogue

The events of recent months had been so bizarre that almost everyone involved wanted to hide them. Although Alan wanted to expose the moral hazard associated with designating as beneficiary someone who would profit more from an insured's premature death than from his continued life, he wasn't sure the best way to go about it. Tony and Alan certainly didn't want to be associated with the murder of a prominent businessman—even a despicable one— therefore publicity about all these events had to be kept to a minimum.

The continuance of DC Capital Life and Fox Investments would be a definite liability to the insurance industry and the viatical settlement industry if their involvement in these premature deaths were to become widely known. It wouldn't do for the public to think of a life insurance policy as a wagering contract and thus be afraid to buy insurance or resell it in time of need.

It was impossible to ignore all that had happened, of course, so the resolution of these problems required a series of compromises:

- DC Capital Life's assets and liabilities were taken over by a consortium of major life insurance companies throughout the country, and the company name was retired. No policyholder lost any value; and any operating losses were spread among the consortium.

- Fox Investments was similarly absorbed

by a consortium of viatical settlement companies, with any operating losses spread among the consortium. Freddy Fox had helped kick start the viatical settlement industry, but his reputation—among insiders at least—was so tarnished that he had to enter another line of business.

- A joint task force was set up by the insurance and viatical settlement industries to develop rules of ethical behavior and compliance enforcement with respect to all viatical settlement operations. Alan Jameson was offered the job as executive director of the task force together with lucrative salary and fringe benefits—provided he sign a confidentiality agreement barring him from publicly discussing the events of recent months.

- Tony Roselle resumed operation of his Club and was more careful in selecting business associates. Alan never visited the Club again, naturally being a little wary of continued association with someone about whom he knew a devastating secret. Tony had offered a monthly stipend to Alan—payable to a confidential account in a Bahamian bank for Alan's remaining lifetime— to ensure that he keep quiet about this secret. In view of what he had recently learned about human behavior and "insurable interest," Alan politely refused this offer.

- Since Tucker Carlton III was dead, it was not possible to learn who had deprived scores of insureds of their natural life spans. In fact, the possibility that these deaths were, in fact, murders was never publicly acknowledged.

As medical advances developed, a diagnosis of HIV/AIDS became a less certain death sentence, and viatical settlements became less common. Eventually the viatical settlement business evolved and was largely replaced by what is termed the "life settlement" business, wherein older people—not necessarily in poor health—sell their life insurance policies to life settlement providers when their economic conditions change or they no longer need life insurance. These life settlement providers then sell the life insurance policies to investment banks or other institutions that pool the policies and securitize them into what has become known as death bonds. Thus the life settlement concept is becoming a wealth management tool ideal for high-net-worth policy owners, resulting in a growing demand for life settlements.

Although in these circumstances the new policy owner/beneficiary is distanced from the insured person, there is still a potential moral hazard because the policy owner/beneficiary has no vested interest in the on-going survival of the insured. Furthermore, these life settlements raised new questions about avoiding fraud and ensuring sound business practices.

These problems could provide challenging work for Alan Jameson for as long as he might care to pursue it. But first he had to decide whether to accept the executive director's job he had been offered, particularly since it entailed a non-disclosure agreement that could be viewed as a bribe for his silence.